Preface

This series of books has been produced for the enjoyment of both children and adults.

They seek to raise awareness of the value of the relationships between pets and people and demonstrate how having a pet enriches your life and family.

Proceeds from the sale of the books will go towards supporting people and pets, by endeavouring to:

- Change the world for one dog at a time with our Rescue, Rehoming and Retirement Program,
- Bringing lonely pets and empty laps together with our Cuddles and Co Program;
- Keeping pets and people together with our Paws and People Boarding and Assistance Program, – and –
- Paying It Pawward with our Program that provides financial assistance to people with pets who are struggling financially

Introduction

Bonsai Ninja is a member of the Hope Springs Gang – a group of small fluffy dogs who have all been adopted when they needed to find a new home. This series of books chronicles their adventures and escapades.

Bonsai is a very small Chihuahua x Pomeranian. But Bonsai has a secret...............

He knows that on the inside he is a very big, very scary German Shepherd

Bonsai just loves life on the farm....

1
BONSAI NINJA
NUMBER 1
SUPER GUY
2
1
3

Bonsai Ninja – (thinks) he's quicker than the Emu's eye

He's super small – but thinks he's super tall
And he thinks he's lightning quick

Don't get in his way - he'll
have something to say And he'll
give you a Ninja Kick!

He has a luscious coat and a lot of style,
And he thinks he's really cool.

He styles his hair with impressive flair,
And a big glob of gooey duck poo!

He likes a belly rub and a lot of love
And the ladies all do sigh –

When there's something he covets,
He turns on the charm, and he gives you the big high five.

If that doesn't work –
he has a nifty trick.

 He gives you the one
eye wink,

He raises the bar with his best high ten
And seals the deal with a bonus lick!

Bonsai Ninja lives a double life. He lives at Hope Springs and is a proud member of the Hope Springs Gang.

He really enjoys dinner time, sitting on the Dogmother's lap, pats (there can never be too many pats), playing with toys that are bigger than he is, and playing chasey with the Dog-Parents

round the house.

He also loves scotch
finger biscuits, licking
the yoghurt container

and burrowing under the
covers of the Dogparent's
bed when it's really cold.

He's not so fond of: the vacuum cleaner, new dogs,

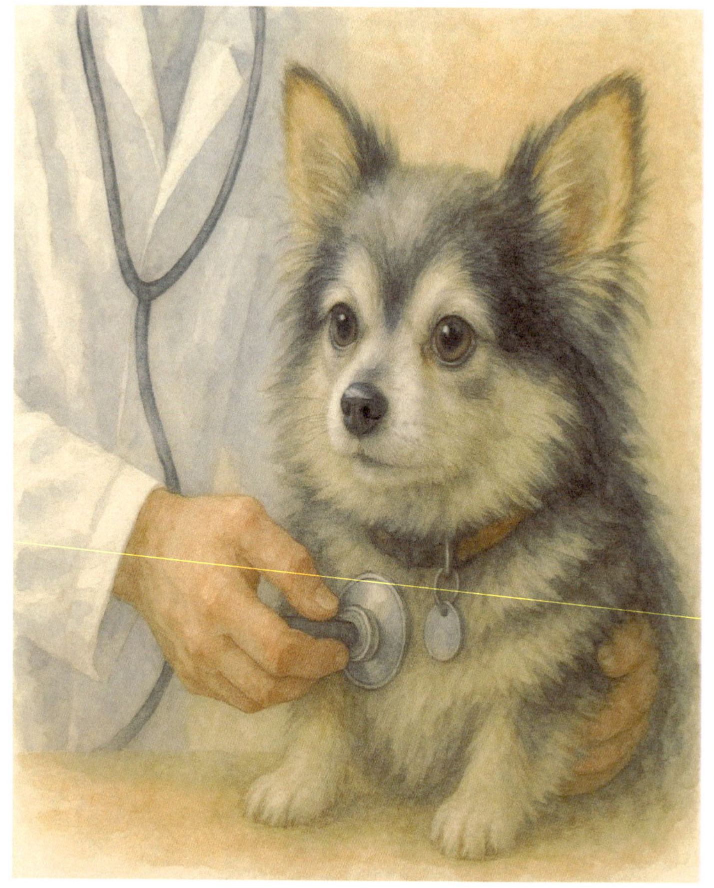

people that come to
visit and going to the
vet.

Bonsai likes to go and bark at the Emu (as long as he has backup), to fossick for possum poo (a doggy delicacy – don't mind if I do) and rolling in duck doo with great enthusiasm!

He loves a good feather!

He's a tiny little guy but he has the courage and the heart of a lion and a spirit as big as the sky!

The family think he's just a super cute, super fluffy, sometimes needy- little dog. But they are wrong!

Totally unknown to his family, Bonsai leads a whole other life – as an international man of mystery.

Cool! Suave! Enigmatic! A ladies' man!

A ninja warrior, a gangsta, he dances Gangnam style, and he was born for the thug lyf! He is – The Bonz!

If only his family knew that the reason he sleeps all day – is because he's living his secret life all night!

Those innocent looking family walks? Entirely contrived
by The Bonz – who is on a ninja mission from DOG himself!
He sniffs out clues, he vanquishes enemies (horses, cows,
alpacas, lambs, kangaroos, rabbits and particularly big
scary people)!

He leaves his signature scent behind – a calling card that whispers: Tuff Guy Was Here!

But the real magic happens when Bonsai falls asleep.

That is when the Bonz truly awakens!

His alter-ego comes to life.

Here's just one of the adventures that occurred while Bonsai slept.

The moon hung over the city like a watchful eye as Bonsai Ninja — The Bonz — padded silently across the marble floor of the Casino Royale.

The doorman, a Great Dane in a tuxedo, nodded respectfully and whispered, "Good evening, Mr. Bonz."

At his side were two glamorous lady dogs, both of similar petite stature, swathed in elegant satin gowns — one shimmering cherry red, the other deep midnight blue.

Diamonds and pearls sparkled at their collars. Together, they made an entrance that turned heads from the baccarat table to the roulette wheel.

The Bonz strolled toward the highstakes lounge, tail held with quiet authority. In shadowed corners, he held secret conversations with other canine spies. A wiry Whippet from the French Bureau de Chien passed him a coded message hidden inside a biscuit. A grizzled Schnauzer from MI9 warned him of "certain elements" in the room — villains in the guise of wealthy patrons. Then... a scent. Danger!!

His ears twitched. His whiskers quivered. With the slightest nod, he signaled the ladies. He had to leave. Moments later, The Bonz was behind the wheel of his cherry-red Lamborghini, engine purring like a contented lion. The night exploded into motion — sleek black sedans in hot pursuit, headlights blazing in his rearview mirror.

A sharp turn.

A daring feint —

Then The Bonz ditched the Lamborghini in a shadowed alley, slipping seamlessly onto a high-powered motorcycle hidden there for precisely such emergencies.

Leather jacket on.

Goggles down. He gunned the engine and vanished into the neon night, leaving his pursuers chewing his dust.

Hours later, mission secure and danger past, The Bonz reclined in the Casino Royale's private lounge, a glass of warm milk by his side. His lady companions lounged beside him, the three of them sharing quiet laughter.

When the evening finally drew to a close, he retired to his very elegant bedroom — silk sheets, velvet cushions, and a monogrammed water bowl by the bed.

Sleep took him quickly.

And when he
awoke.............

  He was back home.
Curled in his familiar
dog bed, the sun
streaming through the
window.

The Dog-Parents
bustled in the
kitchen, blissfully
unaware.

The Bonz smiled to himself. They would never know the intricacies. The risks.

The sheer danger of his real life.

It was better that way. Some secrets are meant to be kept.

After all — he is *Bonsai Ninja*. And he can ninja his way out of *anything*.

TOP SECRET DOSSIER

CODENAME: The Bonz
REAL NAME: Bonsai Ninja
AFFILIATION: Hope Springs Gang
CURRENT LOCATION: Hope Springs, HQ of Fluff Operations
STATUS: Active Agent – International Man of Mystery

LIKES (a.k.a. Motivational Incentives)

- Dinner on the Dogmother's lap
- Pats (unlimited supply required)
- Toys bigger than himself
- Playing chasey with Dog-Parents
- Scotch finger biscuits
- Licking yoghurt containers
- Burrowing under covers on cold nights.
- Barking at the emu
- Styling his hair with duck doo
- Feathers (classified use unknown)

DISLIKES (a.k.a, Known Threats)

- Vacuum cleaner (enemy weapon of mass annoyance)
- New dogs (potential infilitrators)
- Visitors (possible spies)
- Vet visits (probable torture)

SPECIAL SKILLS

- Ninja stealth infiltration
- Gangnam Style dancing (used for distraction and morale)
- Fear deterrence, horses, cows, alpacas, lambs, kangaroos, rabbits, big scary humans
- Heart of a lion, spirit as big as the sky

CLASSIFICATION: HIGHLY CONFIDENTIAL

NOTE: If captured, will deny all knowledge of his double life.

Hope Springs Eternal
DOG RESCUE